SECRETS OF AN OVERWORLD SURVIVOR

JOURNEY TO THE END

GREYSON MANN

ILLUSTRATED BY **GRACE SANDFORD**

Sky Pony Press
New York

Copyright © 2018 by Hollan Publishing, Inc.

Minecraft® is a registered trademark of Notch Development AB.

The Minecraft game is copyright © Mojang AB.

Sky Pony Press books may be purchased in bulk at special discounts for sales promotion, corporate gifts, fund-raising, or educational purposes. Special editions can also be created to specifications. For details, contact the Special Sales Department, Sky Pony Press, 307 West 36th Street, 11th Floor, New York, NY 10018 or info@skyhorsepublishing.com.

Sky Pony® is a registered trademark of Skyhorse Publishing, Inc.®, a Delaware corporation.

Visit our website at www.skyponypress.com.

10 9 8 7 6 5 4 3 2

Library of Congress Cataloging-in-Publication Data

Names: Mann, Greyson, author. | Sandford, Grace, illustrator.
Title: Journey to the end / Greyson Mann ; illustrated by Grace Sandford.
Description: New York : Skyhorse Publishing, [2018]
Identifiers: LCCN 2018001652 (print) | LCCN 2018008922 (ebook) | ISBN 9781510733862 (eb) | ISBN 9781510733848 (pb) | ISBN 9781510733862 (ebook)
Classification: LCC PZ7.1.M366 (ebook) | LCC PZ7.1.M366 Jo 2018 (print) | DDC [Fic]--dc23
LC record available at https://lccn.loc.gov/2018001652

Special thanks to Erin L. Falligant.

Cover illustration by Grace Sandford
Cover design by Brian Peterson

Printed in the United States of America

Interior design by Joshua Barnaby

CHAPTER 1

"Do you think it's going to work?" asked Will, chewing on a fingernail. He watched Mr. Hanson, Little Oak's toolsmith, add more leather to the anvil.

"The lingering potion, you mean?" asked Mina with a faraway look in her green-flecked eyes.

Will threw out his arms. "No! The wing repair!" He had just made the most exciting discovery of his life: a pair of tattered Elytra wings in a treasure chest.

If he could repair them, they would help him glide—no *fly*—across the Overworld!

Mina nodded. "It'll work," she said. "The real question is, will you be able to fly in a straight line?"

He ignored the joke and stared at Mr. Hanson's back. When the toolsmith turned around and wiped his hands on his black apron, Will held his breath. Then Mr. Hanson showed him the Elytra wings. They were pale gray like quartz, perfectly mended, and *beautiful.*

Will could hardly wait to try them out!

"Better practice with these outside," said the toolsmith with a wink. "We don't want you hitting your head on the ceiling."

Will didn't have to be told twice. He thanked Mr. Hanson, took the wings, and darted for the door.

"Will, wait up!" called Mina. "Be careful with those."

He barely heard her. As he strapped on the grey wings, he watched with wonder as they shifted in color, taking on the lapis blue of his cape. Then he raced toward the steep steps of the library. From the top of those steps, he could get a running start.

"Will, wait!" Mina called again.

But he didn't. He sprinted off the top step, spread his wings, and soared. As his wings caught air, he raised his face toward the sky, feeling himself lift higher, higher, higher.

I'm flying! he realized. *Flying!* Like a ghast in the Nether, he soared above the cobblestone well in the middle of Little Oak. And then . . .

He stalled.

And nosedived.

And landed on the ground with a *thud*.

"Oh, no!" He leaped to his feet. "Did I break them?" As he leaned sideways and examined the wings on his back, he was relieved to see that they were still intact.

"Break *them*?" cried Mina as she jogged toward him. "I was afraid you were going to break a leg! Are you okay?"

Will dusted off his pants and wiggled his limbs. "Yeah, but . . . what did I do wrong?"

Mina laughed out loud. "Well maybe you could have asked Mr. Hanson how to *use* the wings before you tried them out." She blew her bangs off her forehead.

"Right," said Will.

Mina was a planner who always slowed down and looked before she leaped. Will usually ran—or flew—full-steam ahead toward the next adventure. *But that's what makes us good partners,* he reminded himself. They'd had adventures all across the Overworld—even in the Nether!

Suddenly, Will had an idea. "We need two pairs of these things," he announced. "One for you and one for me. So we can *fly* to our next adventure!"

Mina hesitated. "You know there's only one place where we can for sure find those wings, right?"

Will's heart began to race. "On an End Ship?"

Mina nodded. "In the End."

Her words hung in the air—like Will had mid-flight, just before his fall.

She licked her lips. "Getting to the End is tough, and even if we *do,* there's only one way back home. We'll have to battle the Ender Dragon and . . ." She looked at him with solemn eyes. "We'll have to *win,* Will."

He kicked at the dirt with his shoe, trying not to think about what would happen if they didn't defeat the Ender Dragon. As he straightened back up, he felt the wings flutter on his back. He *had* to get a second pair for Mina. He had to!

"We went to the Nether and made it out alive," he reminded her.

She shrugged. "The End is even more dangerous than that."

"But we'll have your potions to protect us! And we'll have two pair of Elytra wings. We can practically *fly* home."

Mina played with the end of her ponytail, as if she hadn't heard a word. But Will knew how to persuade her. They'd been friends long enough that he knew *exactly* how to get her on board for this new adventure.

"Just think, Mina," he said, his brown eyes twinkling. "If you fight the Ender Dragon, you can collect some dragon's breath. Then you can brew those *lingering* potions you've been talking about all day. How did you say they work again?"

Her face lit up, and that's when he knew he had her.

"You add them to splash potions," she explained. "Then when you throw the splash potion, it creates this cloud. Any mob that walks through the cloud is affected by the potion!"

Will nodded. "Uh-huh, uh-huh. And have you made any yet?"

She shook her head.

"Why not?"

"I told you!" she said. "I don't have any dragon's breath."

"Exactly."

Mina punched him playfully in the shoulder. "Stop," she said. "I know what you're doing."

But Will knew something, too. They'd be making the journey to the End, even if it was dangerous. Even if they had to battle the Ender Dragon. Because now, Mina wanted to go *just* as badly as he did.

CHAPTER 2

"Here goes nothing."

Will took a deep breath, lowered his head, and sprinted along the top of the obsidian wall. Just before crashing into the redstone torch at the end, he veered left and dove off the wall, spreading his wings for flight.

Down below, his wolf-dog Buddy raced in his shadow, barking wildly.

"I know, girl! I'm flying! Pretty cool, right?"

Will veered left to glide over the pigpens and then right to glide past the garden. His brother Seth's farm looked picture perfect from up here: a black obsidian house surrounded by a bubbling blue moat, a stone gate lit with torches placed at regular intervals, and vegetables planted in straight, tidy rows.

"Oops!" Looking down made Will *fly* downward, too. He glanced up just in time to avoid a face plant in the pumpkin patch.

"Nice save!" called Seth. As he hurried out of the gate, he waved the red and white striped rockets in his hands. "Ready to try a speed boost?"

"Yes!" Will kicked with his legs, eager to land now. Mr. Hanson, the toolsmith, had given him a few tips

yesterday about flying. Number one?
If you want to *fly* instead of glide, you
need to use a firework rocket.

Seth had spent the morning crafting
rockets out of paper and gunpowder—
without stars, he told Will, because those
could blow up right in Will's hand.

"Thanks," said Will as he skidded to a
stop beside his brother. "Those look great!"

"Don't thank me till we find out if
they work," said Seth. He struck a piece
of flint with steel to make a spark. As he
lit the fuse of a fat rocket, a bead of sweat
trickled down his nose.

*He's worried about
me,* Will could tell. Seth
always worried when
Will was about to head

off on another adventure. But he didn't try to talk Will out of it anymore. And sometimes, he even helped Will prepare.

Good old Seth. Will grinned at his brother as he took the lit rocket. Then he set off running along the grass, Buddy at his heels.

A few seconds later, he heard the blast of the rocket and felt the propulsion, lifting him off the ground. Then he was zooming skyward toward the clouds—fast. *Too* fast!

"Look down!" cried Seth from below.

So Will did. But now he was speeding toward the moat! He shifted his gaze back up and tried to level out, but it was too late.

With a splash and a sizzle, he

skidded across the surface of the water. The moat was curving round the bend, but Will *wasn't*. He raced toward the obsidian wall, closer and closer, until finally . . . he sputtered to a stop. *Phew!*

Seth's face popped up over the wall. "Are you okay?" he asked.

A red head appeared beside him. "Sheesh, Will. Another crash?"

Great. Mina always seemed to show up just in time for Will's epic wipeouts.

"Aren't you supposed to be brewing potions?" he grumbled as he stood up in the shallow moat. Water dripped from the tips of his wings, but they were still intact. He flapped them, trying to dry them off.

"I'm done brewing," said Mina. "I've got potions of healing and harming, potions of regeneration, a few golden apples, and some Ender pearls. But we need more pearls—*lots* more—to make Eyes of Ender."

"To activate the End Portal?" asked Will. A shiver ran down his spine, and it wasn't just because he was soaking wet.

Mina nodded. "And to find it in the first place. I mean, we can trade for Ender pearls in town, but we'd need a lot of emeralds. Or—"

"We can *fight* for them," blurted Will. "Endermen drop pearls. We just have to find some of the long-legged mobs!" He tried to sound tough, but the truth was, he hadn't fought a lot of Endermen. There weren't many around Little Oak—not like zombies and creepers, which spawned throughout the village like weeds in a garden.

"We'll have to find about twenty of them," said Mina. "Maybe more." She tapped her chin thoughtfully.

But Will noticed that Seth had fallen strangely quiet. As he polished his steel with the hem of his shirt, he started whistling. "Seth?" asked Will, narrowing his eyes. "What are you hiding? Spill it, brother."

"Huh?" Seth looked up, and then sighed.

"Alright, here's the thing. Endermen spawn like crazy in my mines. I can lead you to a roomful of them any day of the week."

"Today?" asked Will hopefully.

"What's the rush?" asked Seth. Worry lines popped up on his forehead.

"We'll be okay," said Mina with a grin. "I'll bring plenty of potions. I'll protect your little brother." As she jiggled the sack hanging from her shoulder, glass bottles *tinked* together.

Will shot Mina a look as he rounded the wall. "Hey! We both know that *I'll* be the one protecting *you.*"

But Seth didn't even crack a smile. "All I can say is, if you're going to the End, you'd better bring a potion of good luck."

Will snorted. "No such thing."

But Mina held up her finger. "Not so fast. I've heard about a potion of luck, actually."

Will stopped in his tracks. "*Seriously?* Now you tell me? Well, thanks a lot. We sure could have used your potion of luck in the Nether. And when we were battling witches in the swamp. And that time we struck lava in the mineshaft. And—"

"I know, I know," said Mina, "but I just found out about it. I'll try to find the brewing recipe, and I'll meet you both back here this afternoon to hit Seth's mine. But in the meantime, Will?"

"Yeah?"

"You'd better keep working on your gliding." She shot him a smile before heading toward town.

"This way," said Seth. Light flickered on his face from the torches lining the stone corridor.

Will lengthened his stride to keep up with his brother, who knew these mines like the back of his hand.

"How much farther?" Will asked. He heard the *plink, plink, plink* of Mina's potions behind him, which meant she was jogging to keep up, too.

"Down another level," said Seth.

"Where there's even less light." He tightened his grip on his pickaxe and led them down a mossy stone staircase, deeper and deeper into the mine.

When they reached the shadows below, Will reached for his sword. A cave spider could strike at any moment down here. A mob could spawn right before his eyes! "Now what?" he asked Seth.

But Seth just raised his finger to his lips and pointed. Purple dust swirled in a corner of the room.

Then Will heard a grunt.

He whirled around and saw two glowing eyes—two *purple* eyes—glaring at him from out of the darkness.

Will tried to look away, but it was too late!

The Enderman opened its mouth and released an angry, ear-shattering wail.

CHAPTER 3

As the Enderman teleported forward,
Will leaped sideways to dodge the attack.
Then he sliced through the darkness with
his sword. *Aim for his legs!* he reminded
himself. *Don't look up!*

He struck the Enderman's legs
over and over again. With each blow,
the Enderman grunted and stepped
backward. But he kept coming.

And then there were more.

Will saw them step out of the shadows like spiders, their long limbs swishing through the darkness, surrounding Will and Mina. And *Seth*.

Oh, no! Will remembered. His brother was in the room too. And Seth was no fighter.

Will attacked the Enderman with as much strength as he could muster. *Thwack, thwack, thwack!* Again and again, until the Enderman let out one last groan and toppled to the floor.

Something *plinked* to the floor— something green and shiny. An Ender pearl? Will didn't stop to pick it up. There was no time. He had to get to Seth! Where was he?

Will spun in circles, searching the shadowy corners of the room. There! Seth was backed into a corner, battling an Enderman with his pickaxe. And he looked terrified.

Will lunged for the mob and struck him from behind. The Enderman let out a piercing screech and then . . . was gone.

"W-Where'd he go?" asked Seth.

"He teleported," said Mina, breathing hard from her own battle. "But there'll be more. Don't stop. Don't let your guard down."

Will didn't. He stood in front of Seth and battled mob after mob, till his sword felt so *heavy*. Till his arms started to shake. Till he didn't think he could win even one more battle.

Then the room lit up, as if someone had flipped a Redstone switch. And Mina was standing before them with a torch.

"That's enough," she said, panting. "We did it. We got enough Ender pearls." She held up the torch. "Look!"

Beneath Will's feet, the stone floor was littered with pearls—beautiful green, glowing Ender pearls.

"Help me gather them!" she said, opening her sack.

As Will knelt down on shaky legs, he felt his energy flow back and fill his insides like hot lava.

Soon, with the help of these Ender pearls, he'd be battling Endermen again. He'd be exploring a dark world in search of Elytra wings. In the *End.*

Will glanced backward to make sure Seth and Mina weren't looking. They had almost made their way out of the mine, up to Seth's basement, but one long staircase loomed ahead. So Will carefully slid the Ender pearl out of his pocket, took aim, and lobbed it toward the landing at the top of the stairs.

Instantly, he teleported upward, making a wobbly landing on one foot. "Whoa!" He grabbed the wall to steady himself.

"Will, don't waste the pearls!" Mina called from down below.

But he couldn't help it. How could Mina *not* try teleporting? "I wanted to see what it felt like to be an Enderman," he said, laughing.

"How'd it feel?" asked Seth.

"Awesome," said Will. "Like flying." But then he heard a squeak and a scuttle. Something slipped and slid along the landing, inches away from his feet. He jumped backward. "Silverfish!"

But as he reached for a torch, he saw how *black* the mobs

were—purplish black, with glowing red eyes. They sounded like silverfish. They acted like silverfish. But they *weren't* silverfish.

"Endermites," cried Mina as they began tumbling down the steps toward her. "They must have spawned from the Ender pearl!" She dodged a black bug and then drew her sword.

Will did, too. But as his elbow hit the wall, the sword slipped from his fingers! It disappeared over

the side of the staircase and landed
with a *clang* on the cobblestone.

"Was that what I think it was?"
asked Seth.

Will swallowed hard. And nodded
into the darkness.

"Ouch!" As the endermite began
attacking his feet, he kicked at them.
"Get off!" he cried. But the disgusting
critters kept coming.

Then he heard a whine and the
scrabbling of paws on the other side
of the basement door. *Buddy*.

As soon as Will pulled the door
open, Buddy's whiskered snout pushed
through. Then the wolf-dog was on
those endermite like dye on wool. She

snarled, snapping at the bugs—again and again.

Mina and Seth had reached the landing now, too. Together, they and Buddy destroyed the squeaky, scuttling mobs while Will pressed his back against the stone, trying to stay out of the way.

Finally, it was over.

Mina wiped the sweat from her brow with one hand and put the other on her hip. "No more throwing Ender pearls," she said. "We need them! I'm going to craft the Eyes of Ender right now."

"Sorry," said Will. But teleporting *did* kind of feel like flying. So as Mina headed to Seth's crafting table to make Eyes of Ender, he headed back outside to do more flying—with his wings, this time.

He started by climbing onto the stone wall and practicing his gliding again. When Seth lit another rocket, Will held it tightly in his hand and focused on making tiny movements. He glanced gently left or right, or shifted his gaze only *slightly* upward or downward.

By the time the sun started to set over Little Oak, Will knew just where to look on the horizon to get the best hang time—and to avoid nose-dives.

"You've got it!" said Seth, cheering from down below.

But as Will took another turn, he felt his wings losing air. The ground rose suddenly, as if sucking him back downward. "Uff," he said as his feet tripped along the grass. "I must be getting tired."

"Me, too!" called Mina as she came out through the gate. "From crafting.

But, *voila*," she announced, opening her palms. "Blaze powder plus Ender pearls equals Eyes of Ender."

Will hurried over to see for himself. The green Eyes of Ender looked like Ender pearls, except for their fiery glow. "Wow," he breathed. "Very cool."

"So we have what we need," said Mina happily. "We can find the End Portal!"

"You can fly there," said Seth. "At least Will can. You should see him!"

Will puffed out his chest and got ready to show Mina. But as he turned to climb the wall, he heard Seth gasp.

"What?" Will turned around and saw the look of horror on Mina's face, too.

"Your wings," she said, cupping her hands to her mouth. "They're totally tattered!"

CHAPTER 4

Clink, clink, clink!

"That should do it," said Mr. Hanson, turning away from the anvil. "Good as new. *Better* than new." He handed the wings to Will.

They *did* look brand-new. They shimmered with color—every color of the rainbow. "What did you do?" Will asked the toolsmith.

Mr. Hanson winked. "I might have

put the Unbreaking enchantment on
them, to make them extra durable."

"Wow, thanks!" said Will. He
started to strap on the wings.

"Wait," said Mr. Hanson. "Not so
fast. The wings will wear out again
eventually. So you'll want to save them
for when you *really* need them, yes?"
He gave Will a knowing look.

Does he know we're going to the End?
Will wondered as he and Mina left the shop.

"I wish we could take Mr. Hanson's anvil with us," he said to Mina. "So I could repair the wings myself."

She snorted. "An anvil? We couldn't even lift one of those, let alone take it with us. Besides, we'll be taking enough gear. You're wearing your armor this afternoon, right?"

Will nodded—and immediately forgot about the anvil. They were heading into the hills right after lunch to search for the End Portal. And they'd be wearing their armor.

Because if we find the portal, he

thought with excitement, *we're not coming back home any time soon. We're going through it, all the way to the End!*

"You didn't have to come with," Will said again to Seth.

Seth was walking behind Will and Mina, his diamond pickaxe resting on his shoulder. "Sure, I did," he said. "If you find a stronghold with that Eye of Ender, you're going to have to mine down to get to it. So you'll need a miner, and I'm the best guy for the job." He grinned.

Will couldn't argue with that—at

least not without looking away from the Eye of Ender that Mina had just thrown. It soared skyward toward an outcropping of rocks. Then it dropped.

"Did it break?" Mina cried, racing toward the rocks. If it hadn't broken, they could throw the Eye again instead of using another precious one from her supply. "No, there it is!"

As she lobbed the Eye of Ender again, Will fought the urge to flap his wings and fly after it. But he felt so *heavy*. Could

the Elytra even lift him in all this armor?

"How many throws will it take?" he asked. When was that shiny green orb going to finally lead them to the End Portal?

Mina shrugged. "Who knows?"

But her very next throw looked different—shorter. The Eye fell just a few yards away.

"Is your arm tired?" called Seth from behind. "Want me to take a turn?"

Mina shook her head. "The Eye is telling us that we're close now," she whispered.

Will froze and stared at his feet. Was the End Portal right below them?

Seth suddenly sprang into action,

pushing his way past Will. "Show me where to mine," he said.

Soon they were all digging into the earth, hacking through grass, dirt, and stone. But when Seth's diamond pickaxe hit mossy stone brick, he stopped. "This is it," he said. "Careful now."

Will locked eyes with Mina, and they both sat back as Seth began to mine in a zigzag pattern. "Not straight down," he said. "We don't want to fall through."

Soon he had carved out a short staircase toward the stronghold below. But as he started down the steps, Will stopped him. "You should stay here, Seth," he said. "You've got to get all

the way back to the farm before dark!"

He was glad when Seth agreed. But then Seth held out something toward Will—the diamond pickaxe. "Take it," he said. "You might need it."

Will sucked in his breath. "But it's your best one!"

Seth said it again, more firmly this time. "Take it."

So Will did. After giving his brother an awkward hug in his heavy armor, he followed Mina down the mossy steps. When he glanced upward one last time, Seth's worried face still filled the opening.

"Good luck!" called Seth.

Will waved and then stepped into the damp, cool stronghold. For just a moment, he remembered the good-luck potion Mina had talked about. Had she brewed it? He wanted to ask, but she was already too far ahead.

The stronghold was lit by torches—bright enough to see by, but not bright enough to keep mobs from spawning. As Will hurried after Mina down a cobblestone passageway, he scanned the rooms to his right and left for spawners. "Where's the portal?" he called, his voice echoing off the walls.

He saw a flash of Mina's ponytail ahead, and then she darted into a room. Had she found the portal?

Will broke into a run. But as he rounded the corner after her, he saw

that it wasn't a room at all. It was
another corridor. Mina knelt by a
chest on top of a small stone altar. As
the lid to the chest creaked open, she
stuck her head inside.

"A golden apple!" came her muffled
voice. "And bread. And, oh, ha! Look
at this." When she emerged from
the chest, she held something in her

hand. "Ender pearl." She grinned and pocketed the pearl.

"C'mon," Will urged. "This isn't time to look for treasures. Let's find the portal!"

Mina nodded. "I know. I can't help it." She tucked her treasures in her sack and followed Will out of the corridor.

He was in the lead now, and they were getting close—he could *feel* it. His walk turned into a trot, his armor clanking with every step.

He ran past a fountain room on his left. Past a library on his right. He glanced back and saw Mina slowing down, as if the library were pulling her in. But he waved her on. "Mina, c'mon!"

As he rounded the next bend in the

passageway, he saw it—and instantly froze.

Will stood between two narrow pools of lava. Ahead of him, at the top of a stone staircase, was a swirling, spinning silverfish spawner.

But as Will took careful steps to the side, he could see past that spawner. He gazed in wonder at the large green frame, suspended just a few feet above another bubbling pool of lava.

The *End Portal*.

They'd found it. At last!

CHAPTER 5

As Will took another step toward the End Portal, the silverfish spawner came to life. Flames spun, spitting hot sparks through the bars of the iron cage.

"Destroy it!" Mina cried from behind him.

Will was still holding the diamond pickaxe Seth had given him. *You might need it,* Seth had said. And he was right.

Will rushed the spawner, striking it with the pickaxe. He could see the silverfish inside, growing in size, ready to burst outward.

Whack! Will hit it again. The iron cage split. So quickly! Will stared at the diamond axe. "Thank you, Seth," he said out loud.

Then he remembered the portal. Mina was already racing past him. Together, they sprinted up the steps.

"One, two, three . . ." counted Mina. "Three Eyes of Ender are already in place. So we need nine more."

Will leaned forward. Sure enough, some of the blocks of the green portal frame held glowing Eyes of Ender. He helped Mina place the others, careful not to drop them into the lava—or to fall into it himself.

"Last one," said Mina, holding up the Eye. "You ready?"

Will nodded and held his breath.

As Mina dropped the Eye of Ender into place, the lava beneath the portal disappeared. The frame was suddenly filled with . . . darkness. Twinkling lights, like stars in the sky, beckoned to Will.

"Wait!" cried Mina. "The Ender dragon

is on the other side, Will. Are you ready?"

He swallowed hard. He tightened his armor around his chest and reached for his sword. Then he nodded.

Mina took a deep breath. "Okay."

Before Will could even see it coming, she dove—headfirst—into the dark portal.

"Wait!" he cried, tumbling in after her.

But the nothingness sucked his voice right out of his throat. He spun, feeling weightless—even in his heavy armor.

Then the world stopped spinning, and he was staring into the darkness of the portal again. Except it *wasn't* the portal. It was the night sky—a starless sky.

Mina's face appeared above him. "Get up!" she cried, reaching for his hand.

As she pulled him upward, he looked

down—and gasped. They stood on the edge of a platform that teetered high above the earth. The island below had

an eerie greenish glow.

"We have to find a way across," said Mina, pacing the edge of the platform. "The Ender dragon will be there, near those pillars."

She pointed toward the island, which held a ring of tall black pillars. But between the platform they were perched on and the island below, there was nothingness—an endless black void.

"We can't fall," whispered Mina. As she pointed downward, her hand shook.

"We can fly!" said Will, suddenly remembering his wings.

"You can," said Mina. "But . . ." Her voice trailed off.

Now Will started pacing, too. "See?"

he said. "This is why we need another pair of wings. Or another way to fly."

The answer struck him like a lightning bolt. "That's it! Ender pearls—another way to fly. You can throw an Ender pearl," he said to Mina. "Like I did in Seth's mine."

"All the way over there?" asked

Mina, pointing toward the island.

Will nodded. "You can do it!" he said. "I watched you throw the Eyes of Ender. You have a good arm—you throw pretty far. Unless you want me to . . ."

The spark returned to Mina's eyes. "No, I can do it."

Will blew out a breath of relief. The truth was, he wasn't sure he *could* throw that far!

But as Mila wound her arm back, he knew she could. She launched the pearl skyward until it disappeared from view. And then Mina did, too.

"Wait!" cried Will. He tightened his wings on his back and looked downward. Could he glide that far? Maybe not. He pulled a firework

rocket from his pack and lit it, hoping
Mina had made it to the island—
hoping he'd see his friend again.

The rocket sizzled to life, and then
Will did the only thing he could do.
He jumped.

As the rocket ignited, it pulled him forward. His stomach dropped as he soared through darkness, toward the island in the distance. *Don't panic,* he told himself. *You practiced this. You know how to fly!*

So he kept his gaze straight ahead, aiming for the black pillars. As he got closer, he looked downward—just slightly—to prepare to land.

That's when he saw something else.

Something with dark, shadowy wings.

Something with a long barbed tail and glowing purple eyes.

Something flying *straight* toward him.

CHAPTER 6

Will veered left to avoid the dragon. He swooshed past an obsidian pillar, missing it by only inches.

He desperately wanted to turn his head, to search the dark skies for the dragon. Was it coming back? Was it right behind him?

But he couldn't look! If he did, he'd fly in circles—or spiral downward to certain death.

So instead, Will stared straight ahead, setting his sights on the end-stone runway ahead. He saw a shadowy cluster of long-legged Enderman in his path, but he didn't care. Endermen, he could handle. After all, he had just come face to face with the Ender Dragon himself.

Will looked left, only slightly, to veer past the Endermen, making sure to avoid their glowing eyes. Then he braced himself for impact. As his feet skidded along the end stone, he saw sparks fly.

When he finally came to a stop, he scanned the sky, searching for the dragon. He couldn't see a thing in the darkness, but he suddenly heard the swoop of massive wings.

Then he heard a cry. "Will!"

It was Mina—she was here! She had made it. Will took a shaky breath of relief and then called back. "Where are you?"

"Here!" She stood at the base of a pillar, her bow and arrow drawn.

Will half ran, half glided toward her. When he reached her side, she crouched low and glanced around the side of the pillar.

"It's making laps," said Mina. "I shot it once, but it's healing itself."

"The dragon?" asked Will.

She nodded. "The crystals on top of the pillars give it strength."

Will glanced up just as a beam of light shot from a pillar, casting a purple spotlight on the claw-footed dragon. In that instant, he saw the dragon change course. It swooped downward— straight toward Will and Mina.

"Duck!" cried Mina.

Except she didn't. Will saw her pull back the string of her bow and release an arrow, right into the face of the dragon.

As her arrow struck its target, the dragon let out a mighty roar. Hot breath and a cloud of purple poison spewed from its mouth. Will flattened himself onto his stomach and tried not to breathe in the poison.

But Mina rushed straight into the purple cloud, gathering it in a glass bottle. *Dragon's breath,* thought Will—the treasure Mina had come for.

"You hit him!" he cried when she finally squatted down beside him. "You got him straight in the face."

"It doesn't matter," said Mina, covering her mouth. "He'll heal himself. We have to shoot out the crystals." As she put the dragon's breath into her pack, she pulled out her healing potion and took a quick swig. Then she raised her bow and arrow. "Help me!" she cried.

Will tried. He aimed his arrow at one of the crystals. But it was so far away! And he was way better with his sword than with his bow.

As Mina hit the first crystal, it exploded, sending shards of light and glass flying. *Boom!* she hit a second crystal. And a third.

Will tried again—and missed.

Then Mina set down her bow. "I can't get that one!" she said, pointing. "I think it's in an iron cage."

Will squinted to see. Sure enough, one of the crystals seemed protected by the cage around it. The cage looked like a spawner—a silverfish spawner.

And Will knew exactly how to take care

of that. But he suddenly couldn't move.

"What?" asked Mina, noticing the look on his face.

So he told her. "I could fly up and break the cage. It's the only way. But . . . Don't you have like a potion of courage or something?"

She laughed. "No, I'm fresh out."

"Wait! Did you brew the potion of luck?"

Mina hesitated. Then she dug through her bag. "You mean this?" She held out a vial of blue liquid.

"Yes!" Will grabbed it, unscrewed the lid, and guzzled it down. Instantly, he felt better. And braver.

"Don't worry," he told Mina. "I've got this."

He reached into his own sack for another firework rocket and some flint and steel. As he lit the fuse of the rocket, he glanced up at the pillar.

Could the rocket send him that high in the sky? Maybe, if he looked upward. If he didn't stall.

I drank the potion of luck, he reminded himself. *I won't stall.*

As the rocket burst in his hand, he shot upward. He kept his eyes trained on the caged crystal, hoping, hoping, hoping he could reach it and not sail on by.

It grew closer and closer—the brilliant light blinding him. And then he started to slow.

"No," he said, kicking his legs. "NO!"

He felt the stall coming, but instead of glancing down, he lunged toward the crystal and threw out his pickaxe. The sharp edge of the tool caught the iron cage, and then Will was dangling by one arm, the weight of his body pulling him downward.

"Will!"

He couldn't look down at Mina. If

he did, he'd see just how high he was above the ground—and how far he might fall.

Instead, he swung his body just a little. Just enough so that his other hand could grip the top of the obsidian pillar. It felt cool and firm beneath his fingertips, but also a bit slippery.

Don't panic.

He found a fingerhold and began to pull himself up, the muscles in his arms shaking. Now, finally, he could grip the cage with his hand and swing his leg over the side.

Then he was standing over the crystal.

When he heard the swoop of a dragon's wing, he kicked into action.

He raised the pickaxe high in the air and brought it down hard.

He missed the cage. But the blade of his axe slipped through the iron bars and hit the crystal.

The world exploded with light, but Will didn't hear a *boom.* Instead, everything went silent.

And very, very dark.

CHAPTER 7

When Will came to, his head throbbed. And fireworks exploded in the sky above him—bursts of light in a purple sky.

"Are those Seth's rockets?" he asked. But he could barely hear his voice. It sounded so far away.

"It's the [something, something]," Mina said. She was in front of him now, but she looked blurry, as if she were underwater.

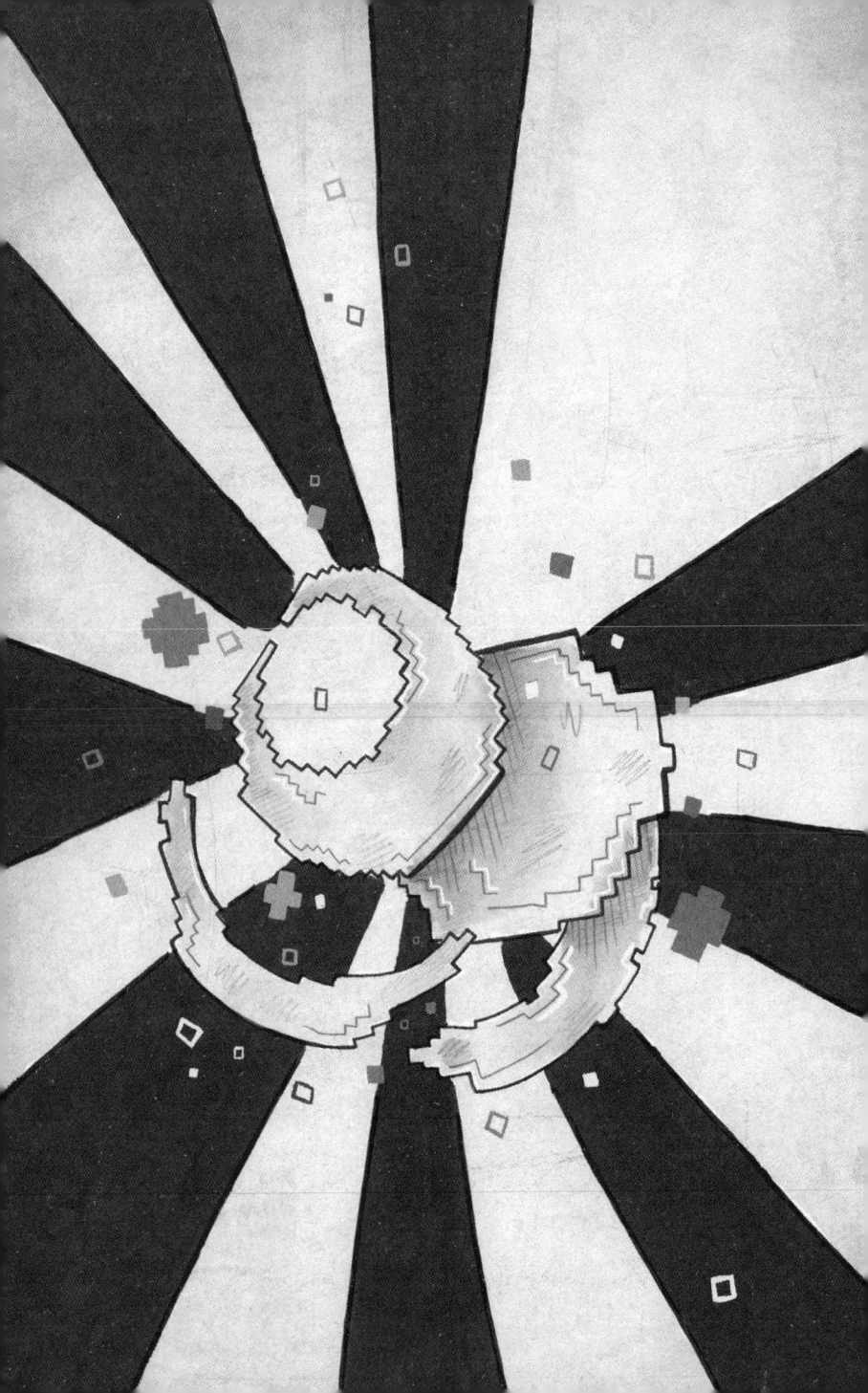

"The what?"

"The Ender Dragon," Mina said, louder this time. "We killed the dragon! You destroyed the last crystal, Will, and then I took the dragon down with my arrows."

Will sat up fast—too fast—and the dark, eerie world around him began to spin. He remembered now. They were in the End. He had tried to destroy a crystal. He *had* destroyed the crystal, but . . . it had almost destroyed him.

"Did I fall?" he asked Mina.

She hesitated, and then nodded. "But your wings saved you—they slowed your fall," she said.

"Your potion of *luck* saved me,"

he corrected her. Then he felt for his wings, but couldn't find them.

"There," said Mina, pointing.

When he followed her gaze, Will's stomach sank. His beautiful wings were  lying beside him, bent and broken, tattered and torn.

"So much for getting you some Elytra wings and flying home together," he said, sinking back down.

"It's okay," said Mina. "We don't need wings to fly home. We'll take the Exit portal." She pointed toward a bedrock pillar lit by torches. "When the dragon died, he activated the portal. And that one, too—the End Gateway to End Cities and Ships." She gestured toward a cluster of rocks suspended in the air a few feet above them.

"But you brewed me a potion of luck and everything!" said Will sadly. "And I couldn't even get you your wings."

Mina held up her hand. "Alright, Will. Enough about the potion of luck already."

"Just saying . . ." he mumbled.

"Without that, I probably wouldn't even be here."

Mina let out an exasperated sigh. "Yes, you *would*. You would have done fine on your own. You did do fine on your own. Will, I didn't give you any potion of luck."

"Huh?"

She looked away, the way Buddy did whenever she'd done something wrong. Will suddenly missed that dog.

"Turns out, you can't brew potion of luck—at least not yet," said Mina. "You have to find it in treasure chests. But you kept going on and on about how much you *needed* it, just like you needed another pair of Elytra wings."

She was kind of going on and on now, too, her words spilling out like scuttlefish from a wall.

"So you *lied* to me?" he said, giving her a hard stare. "What potion did I drink?"

She laughed nervously. "Awkward potion. Plain old awkward potion. It doesn't do a thing."

Will suddenly felt like spitting. "I drank straight-up Nether wart?" he asked.

She shrugged. "The point is, you didn't need potion of luck or any good-luck charm. You flew up to the top of that pillar all on your own. All you needed was a little courage and your own skills."

As Will pictured himself dangling

from that crystal cage by the pointy end of a pickaxe, his hands started to sweat. And red-hot anger began spinning in his chest. "I could have died falling from that pillar!"

"I know," said Mina in a small voice. "But we would have died anyway if you hadn't flown up there. The Ender dragon would have kept coming at us."

She had a point, but Will sure wasn't going to admit it. He jumped to his feet. "I'm going home," he said, heading toward the Exit portal.

But after only two steps, his legs gave out.

So when Mina handed him a vial

of healing potion, he drank it. He ate the Golden Apple she offered, too, even though he wasn't the slightest bit hungry.

By the time he finally marched off toward the Exit portal, he didn't feel quite so mad anymore. And he still wanted those Elytra wings. Maybe he didn't *need* them, anymore than he'd needed that potion of luck. But he really, really wanted them.

So halfway toward the pillar of the Exit portal, he turned and walked back toward the End Gateway instead. If he wanted to find Elytra, he had to first find an End Ship.

But as he approached the cluster

of rocks suspended in the sky,
he scratched his head. How were
they supposed to get through it?
The gateway in the middle of the
bedrock looked so small! Then he
remembered—and he had to speak to

Mina, even if he didn't want to. "Do you have any more Ender pearls?"

Her face lit up. "Yes!" She dug a few out of her sack and jogged toward Will, her hand outstretched.

The first pearl he threw bounced off the bedrock and broke on the end stone below. But the second pearl passed through.

And so did Will.

The End Gateway was behind him now, glowing a deep shade of purple. And Will was surrounded by tall creepy trees—purplish trees that reminded him of Endermen. He shivered, and was grateful when Mina suddenly appeared beside him.

"Chorus plants!" she cried. "I've heard about these." She rushed toward one of the purple trees and started plucking flowers from the top.

Will prickled at her perkiness. *Doesn't she know I'm still mad at her?* he wondered.

He started walking, but toward what? All he could see for miles around were glowing green end stone and purple trees. And occasionally, an Enderman.

But he kept walking, checking back every so often to be sure Mina was still there.

Is it day or night? he wondered. It all seemed the same here in the End— dark and mysterious.

But when Mina shrieked from behind him, he woke as if from a dream.

She was pointing toward something massive in the distance. Something magical. A purple tower rose above them, branching like the biggest treehouse Will had ever seen.

"An End City!" cried Mina. And she started to run.

CHAPTER 8

"Watch out for shulkers," Mina whispered as they tiptoed through the lower room of the End City tower. "They're purple."

Will snorted—he couldn't help it. *Everything* in this room was purple, because everything was made from purpur building blocks. He passed purpur pillars and purpur slabs as he followed Mina up a purpur staircase.

The bottom room opened up into a larger one, and then another. But as Will and Mina began winding their way up a tower staircase, the steps became farther apart. Will had to leap from one to the next.

"Don't fall!" cried Mina looking down.

Will knew better than to look down—he'd learned that lesson already. So he hurried past Mina and took the lead.

At the top of the tower, rooms branched off to the right and left. "Treasure chests!" Will called down, knowing Mina would want to check out the loot here in the End City.

He heard her footsteps on the stairs as he explored the first room. Two chests sat side by side, and end rods lit the room like torches. Was that a chandelier hanging from the ceiling?

Will glanced up—just as the purpur block hanging above him cracked opened. From the white mass within, two eyes stared back at Will.

"Shulker?" he whispered.

"Shulker!" Mina cried from behind. "Shoot it!" She raised her bow and arrow, but the shulker snapped its shell shut. Her arrows pinged off the purple shell as if it were a diamond shield.

Then the shell spun open again. "Hit it!" cried Mina.

Will trained his own bow on the white mob. But as he pulled back his arrow, the shulker took aim, too—and fired.

Suddenly, a white missile was barreling toward Will.

As he dodged left, he watched in horror as the bullet dodged, too. It circled back around, following his every move.

"What now?" he cried, racing for the stairs.

"Hit it!" Mina cried. "With your sword!"

Will drew his sword and swung wildly at the white bullet. He missed, then swung again and struck the bullet, sending it sailing backward. "Yes!"

But the shulker kept firing.

One missile sizzled toward Mina. Two more wound their way toward Will. While he was smacking the first, the second one struck his armor and knocked Will right off his feet.

Suddenly he was levitating above the staircase—above the roof of the End City!

He reached back to feel for his wings, and then remembered he had destroyed them. His mouth went dry.

"Mina!" he cried.

She popped her head through the hole in the roof. "Don't move," she called. "Stay above the rooftop. When the levitation wears off, you're going to fall."

Barely two seconds passed before Will felt the world drop out from beneath him. He was falling alright, but he was smiling, too.

Because Will had just spotted something floating in the sky on the *other* side of the End City.

Something with a bow and a mast.

An End Ship!

"Are you sure you're okay?" asked Mina as she handed him an Ender pearl.

"More than okay," he said. Sure, his leg hurt from that sudden drop onto the End City rooftop. But he was only *minutes* away from finding the Elytra wings now.

He wound his arm backward and launched the Ender pearl. Did it bounce on the deck of the ship? He couldn't tell, but suddenly he was *standing* on that ship—waiting for Mina.

She appeared beside him with her bow and arrow drawn. "There'll be more shulkers," she said. "Be ready."

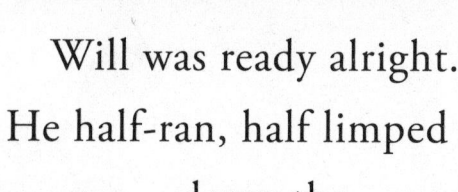

Will was ready alright. He half-ran, half limped down the length of the ship, searching for a staircase.

There! He took the stairs two at a time, practically flying.

The first thing he saw in the room below was a brewing stand. Mina saw it, too. "Wait!" she cried. "Let me brew a lingering potion—I have the dragon's breath now."

But Will couldn't wait. He left her there, digging vials out of her sack, as he raced down a long corridor to the other end of the ship.

Then he saw them.

Gray, glorious wings hanging in a frame above two treasure chests. The Elytra practically glowed in the light of the end rod projecting from the wall above.

Will lunged toward the wings—until he saw the purpur block perched on the treasure chest below. But it wasn't purpur. As the block cracked open, Will sucked in his breath and took a step backward.

"Mina!" he called. "Shulkers!"

"I'm almost done," she cried. "Wait for me!"

This time, Will did. He had to! The shulker was right

below the Elytra. What if Will's arrow missed the shulker and hit the wings?

He was going to need Mina's help on this one. So he darted behind a wall, hoping not to antagonize the shulker. And he waited.

Finally Mina emerged from the brewing room with a bubbling vial in her hands. "Lingering potion," she said with a satisfied smile.

Then her eyes widened and she ducked. A missile steamed overhead, nearly parting the red hair on her head. "The shulker's firing!"

As she drew her bow, Will leaped out from behind the wall. "Don't hit the Elytra!" he cried.

"I won't. You hit the missile and I'll hit the shulker," she said. "Hurry!"

Will drew his sword and searched the room for the missile. He'd have to cut it off in its path *before* it struck Mina. There, in the corner! The white bullet rounded the bend and veered toward Mina.

But Will got to it first. *Whack!* He sent the bullet sailing backward.

Then he heard the *thwang, thwang, thwang* of Mina's arrows. "Got it!" she cried.

As Will raced into the treasure room, Mina was collecting the shulker shell that had dropped to the floor. And now Will had a clear path to those wings.

He didn't run—he walked. Carefully. And he gently took them down from the wall.

These Elytra were brand-new. "They've never been worn before," he said under his breath.

But Mina heard him. "Maybe it's time," she said. "C'mon!"

She led him up to the deck of the ship. As they stood near the rail, she asked, "Are you ready to fly home—or at least back to the End Gateway?"

Will shook his head.

"You're *not*?" she asked.

"Nope," he said with a smile. "*You* fly this time. These wings are for you."

Mina took the wings from him as if they were a precious potion. As she slid her arms through the straps, the Elytra turned emerald green, her favorite color.

But as she climbed the deck rail, she hesitated. "Do you think I can fly a straight line?" she asked, chewing her bottom lip.

"Sure!" said Will. "I know you can. Just don't look down!"

She took a deep breath. "Okay. Wish me luck."

"Nope," said Will. "You don't need it. You've got skills—and smarts."

Mina looked back at him and laughed out loud. "Nope. We don't need luck. Because we have each other. Right?"

"Right."

Will watched his friend leap into the darkness. Then he threw an Ender pearl into the void beyond—and followed her.